Bruno's

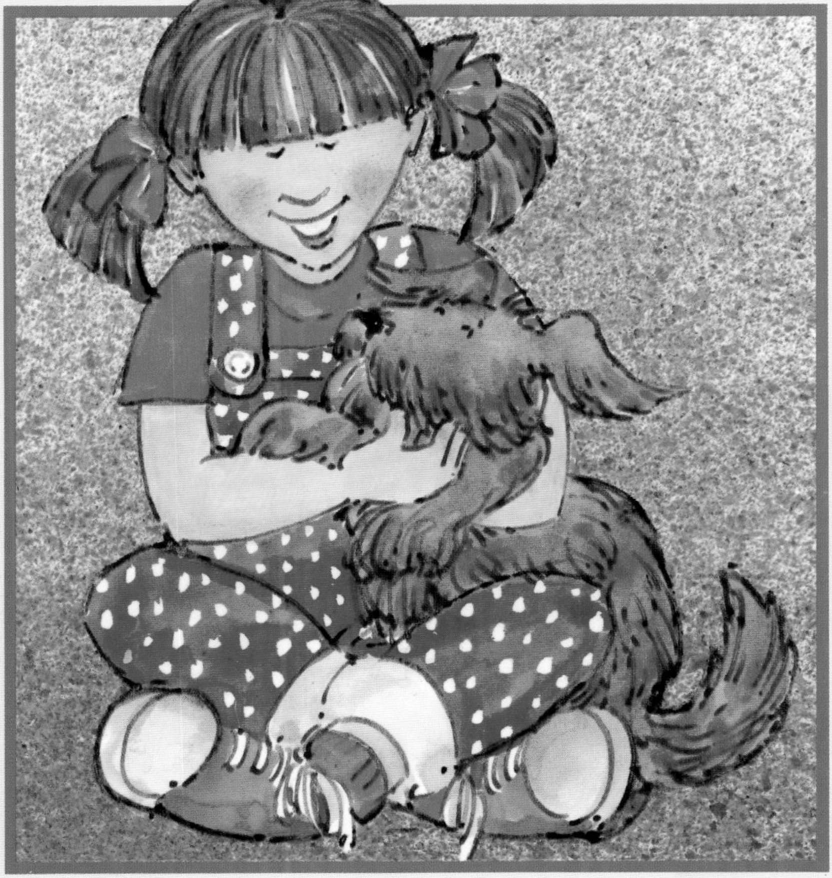

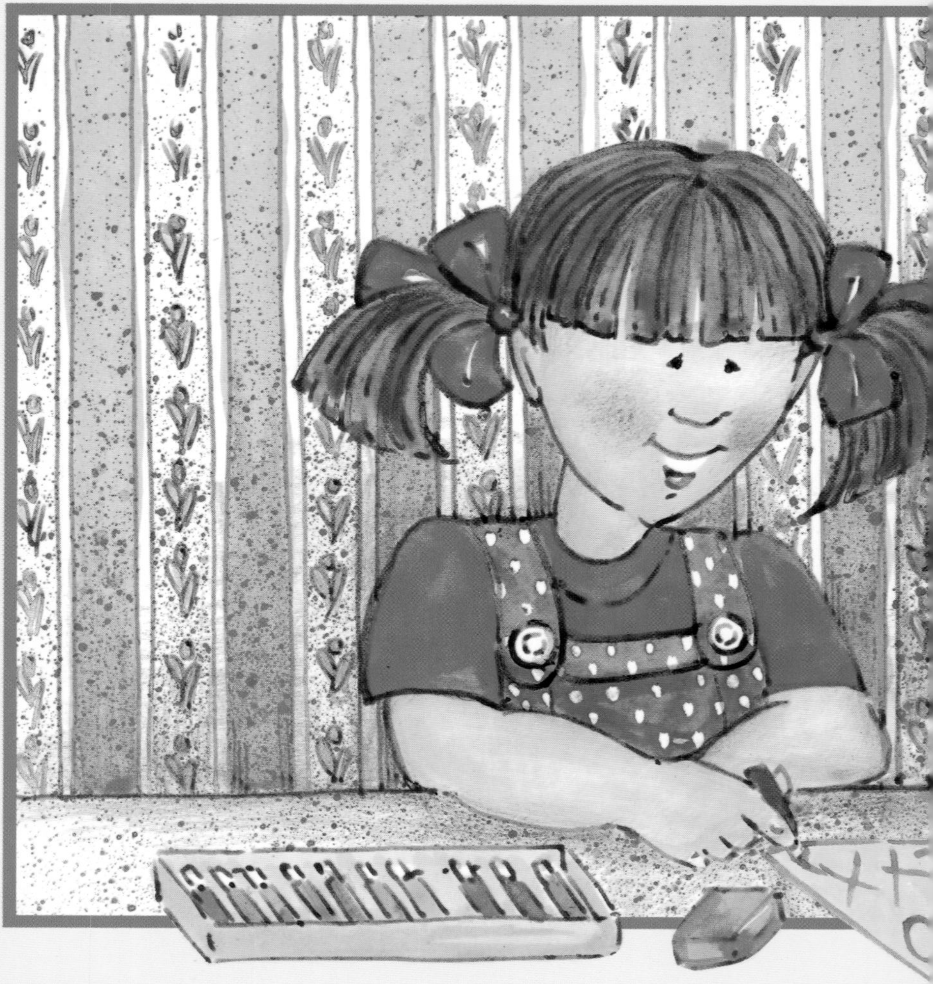

Today is Bruno's birthday.

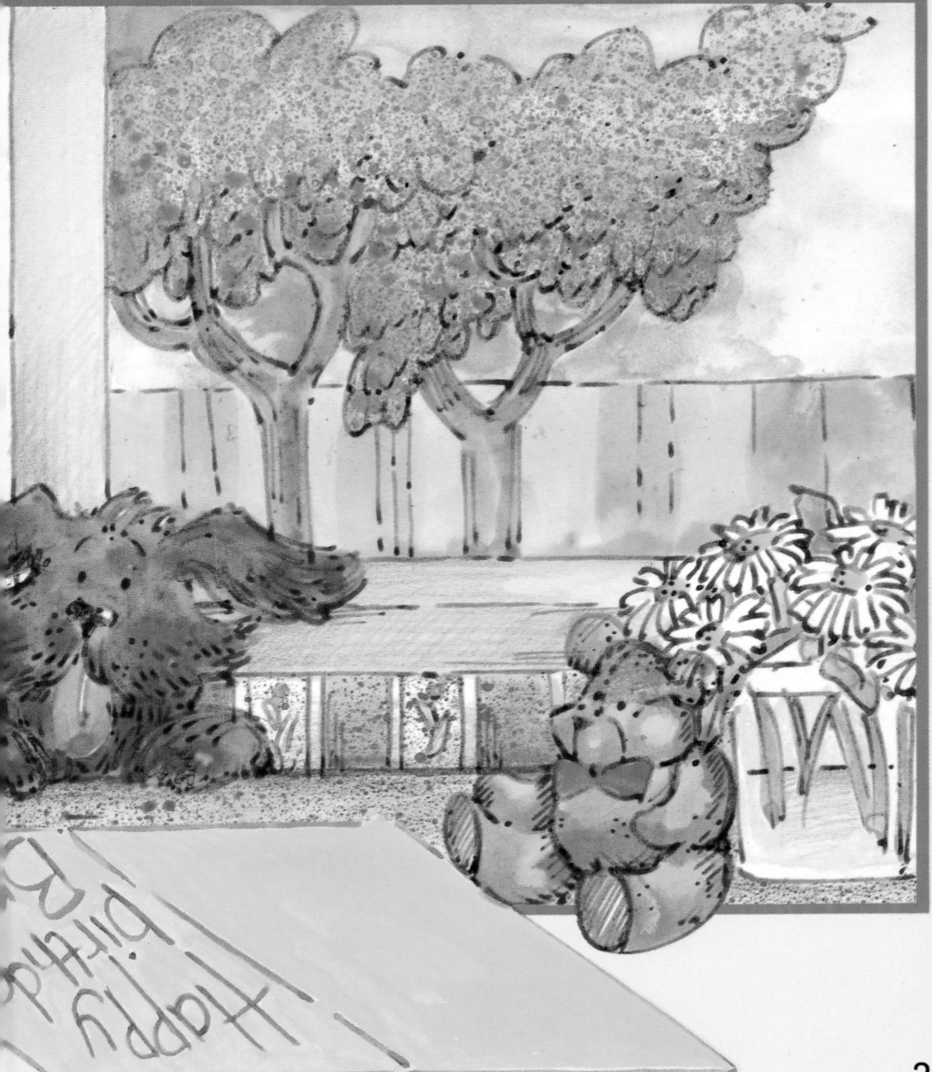
Happy

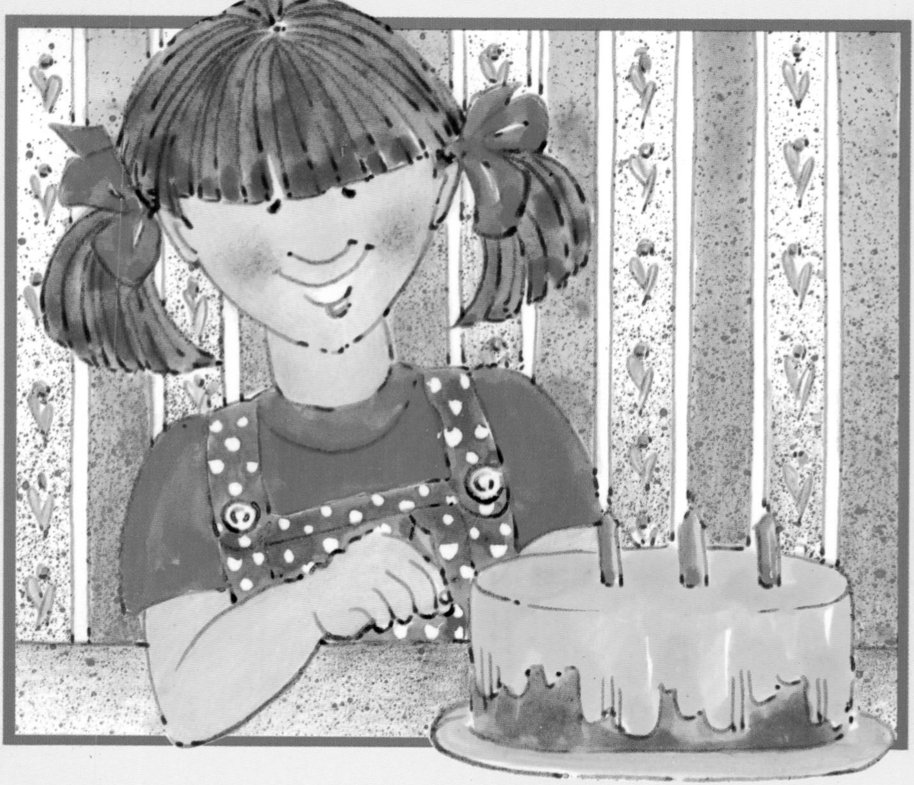

He has a cake
with four candles.

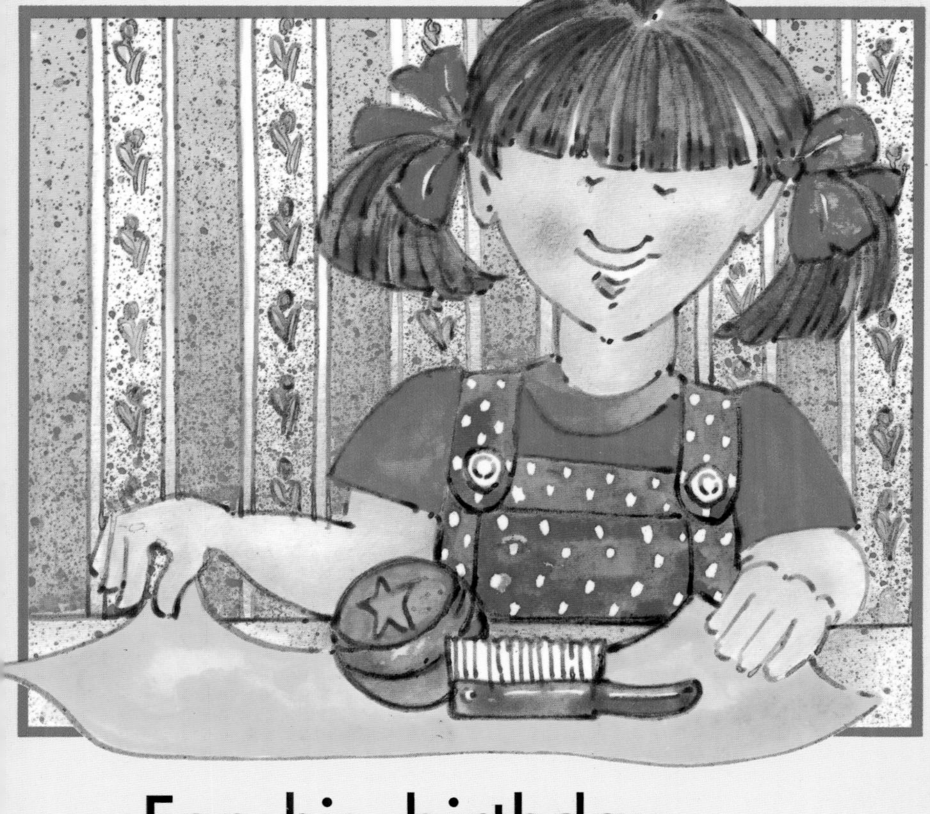

For his birthday,
Bruno is getting
a brush and a ball.

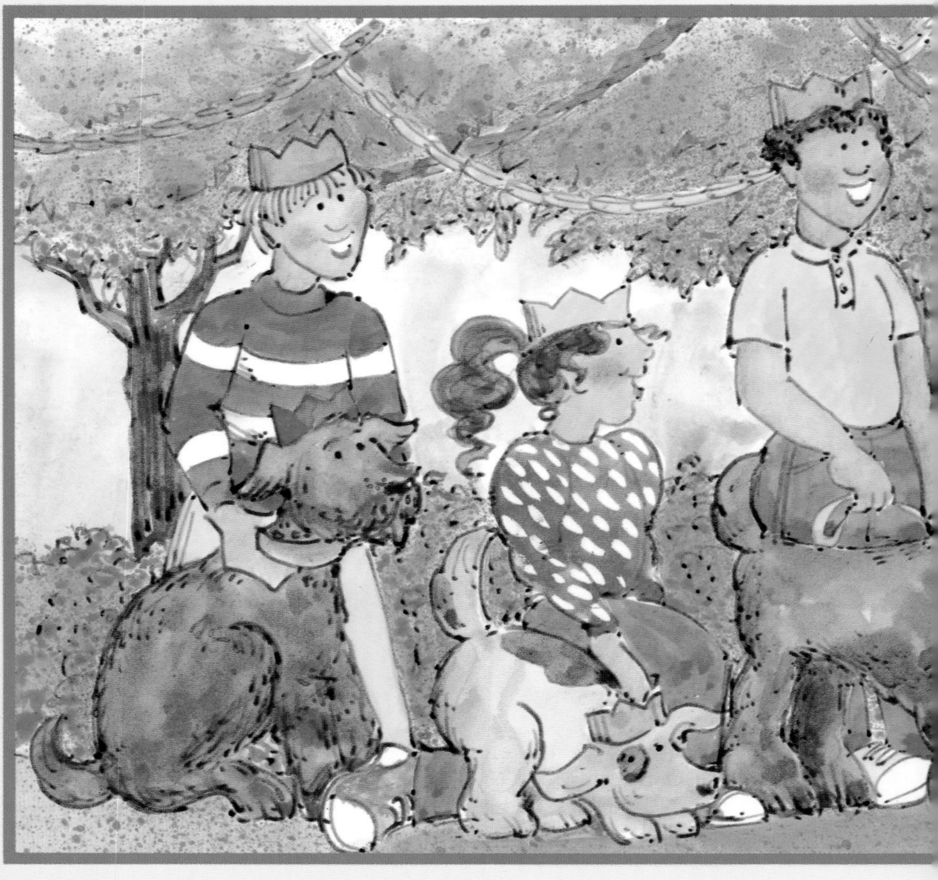

Bruno's friends are coming to his party.

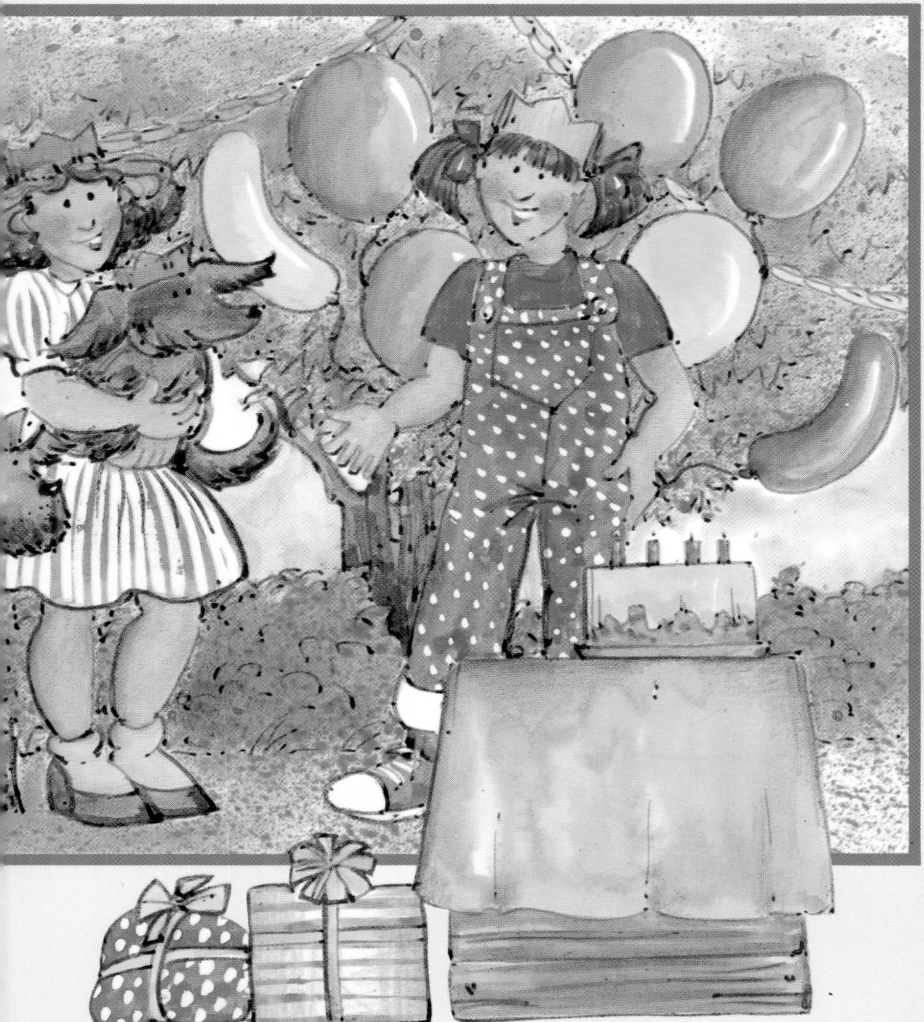

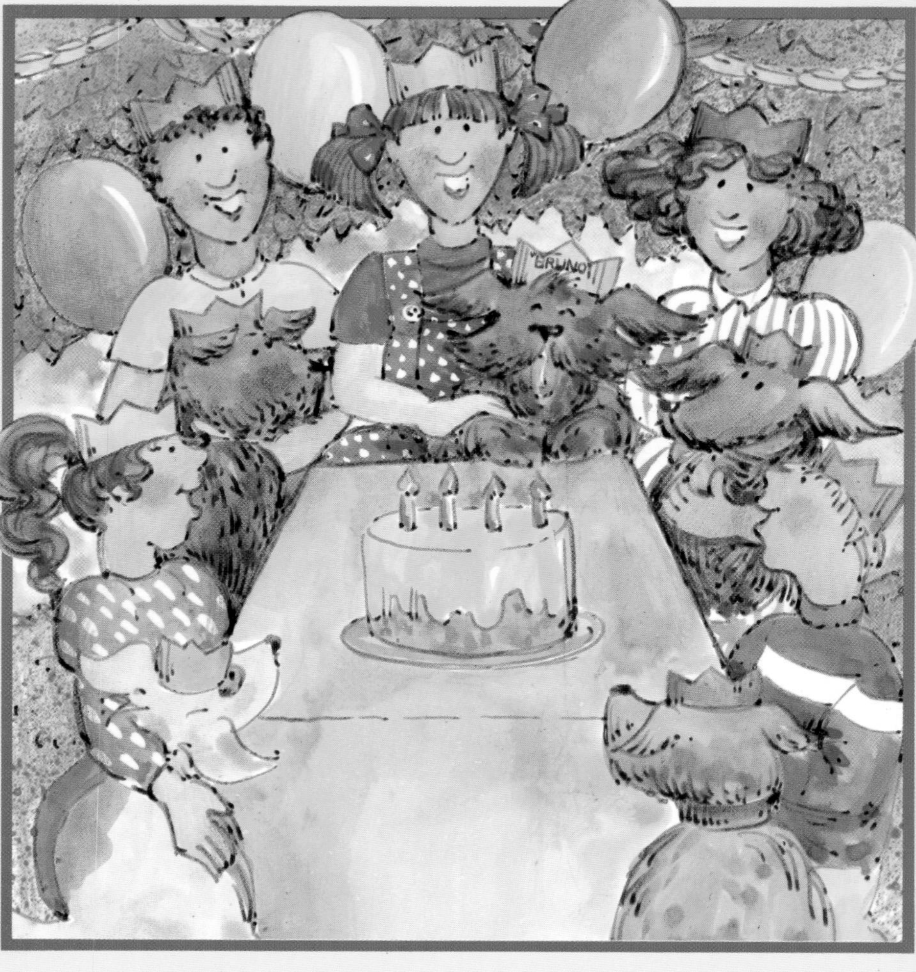

"Happy Birthday, Bruno!"